A STOLEN SPORK!

"I'm afraid we have a problem," Mr. Roberts announced. "Morpho's Morph Spork is missing!"

"Oh no!" Joe exclaimed. He couldn't believe his ears. How could the Morph Spork be missing?

Everyone else was surprised too. Just about the whole audience started talking at once.

"This is terrible," Phil said. "Morpho's nothing without his Spork!"

THE HARDY BOYS® SECRET FILES

#1 Trouble at the Arcade

#2 The Missing Mitt

#3 Mystery Map

#4 Hopping Mad

#5 A Monster of a Mystery

THE HARDY BOYS®

SECRET FILES #5

A Monster of a Mystery

BY FRANKLIN W. DIXON

ILLUSTRATED BY SCOTT BURROUGHS

ALADDIN · NEW YORK LONDON TORONTO SYDNEY

ALADDIN

An imprint of Simon & Schuster Children's Publishing Division
1230 Avenue of the Americas, New York, NY 10020
First Aladdin paperback edition April 2011
Text copyright © 2011 by Simon & Schuster, Inc.
Illustrations copyright © 2011 by Scott Burroughs
All rights reserved, including the right of reproduction in whole or in part in any form.
ALADDIN is a trademark of Simon & Schuster, Inc., and related logo is a registered trademark of Simon & Schuster, Inc.
THE HARDY BOYS is a registered trademark of Simon & Schuster, Inc.
For information about special discounts for bulk purchases, please contact Simon & Schuster Special Sales at 1-866-506-1949 or business@simonandschuster.com.
The Simon & Schuster Speakers Bureau can bring authors to your live event.
For more information or to book an event contact the Simon & Schuster Speakers Bureau at 1-866-248-3049 or visit our website at www.simonspeakers.com.
Designed by Lisa Vega
The text of this book was set in Garamond.
Manufactured in the United States of America 0311 OFF
10 9 8 7 6 5 4 3 2 1
Library of Congress Control Number 2010929189
ISBN 978-1-4169-9166-3
ISBN 978-1-4424-1987-2 (eBook)

CONTENTS

1   MONSTER ATTACK!   1

2   A HORRIFYING PLAN   10

3   WAITING IN LINE   20

4   MEETING MORPHO   29

5   WHERE'S THE SPORK?   38

6   LOOKING FOR SUSPECTS   45

7   ANOTHER MYSTERY   53

8   SIDETRACKED   61

9   MASK ATTACK   69

10 SECRET FILE #5: A SURPRISING
    SOLUTION   81

1

Monster Attack!

F aster!" Frank Hardy shouted.

His brother, Joe, bent over the handlebars of his bike, pumping as hard as he could after Frank. Their bikes flew up a hill and jumped off the far side, landing on the dirt trail below.

"He's coming!" Iola Morton shrieked, glancing over her shoulder. She was riding her bike beside Frank's.

"We have to get away!" their other friend, Phil Cohen, yelled from his bike.

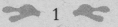

"Go! Go!" Joe urged.

All four of them sped around a curve in the trail. They were deep in the woods behind Bayport Park. It was pretty wild back there, with lots of winding trails and hills. It was a fun place to ride bikes—at least, when there wasn't something scary chasing you.

Just then there was a terrifying roar from somewhere behind them.

"It's the Morph Monster!" Iola cried. "He's catching up!"

Joe pedaled even faster. "If he catches us, we're dead meat!" he yelled to the others. "He'll eat our brains and take over our identities!"

"Yeah. Then he'll go eat all our friends and families too!" Phil exclaimed.

He skidded around a sharp bend in the trail. Frank and Iola were right behind him.

Joe started to follow the others. But the trail

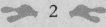

was a little bit muddy here. His friends' tires had gouged a rut in the dirt when they spun around the bend. Before he knew what was happening, Joe's front tire got stuck in the rut. The handlebars twisted out of his grip, and Joe went flying.

"Ow!" he yelped as he hit the rocky ground.

His hands and knees scraped painfully on the

dirt, but he hardly noticed. He was back on his feet a second later.

"Hey!" he yelled to his brother and their friends. "Wait up!"

But they were already out of sight around the bend. Joe could barely hear them calling to one another as they rode away.

Gritting his teeth, he yanked his bike free of the mud. Then he jumped back on and tried to ride after them. But the front wheel wouldn't move, and Joe almost ended up on the ground again.

"Oh no!" he muttered.

Now he saw that the front wheel was twisted. It must have happened when he crashed.

"Guys!" he shouted, louder this time. "Come back! The Morph Monster is going to get me!"

"ROAAAAAAAAR!"

Joe winced. It was too late! He spun around . . . just in time to see his friend Chet Morton ride into the clearing. Chet was wearing a scary monster mask over his bike helmet.

"I got you, Joe!" Chet cried gleefully. His voice sounded muffled behind the rubber mask. "I'm Morpho, and I'm going to eat your brains!"

"Yeah, yeah," Joe said with a sigh. "You got me, okay? Now come help me fix my bike."

Chet dropped his bike and pushed back his mask. His round cheeks looked extra pink from being under it.

"What's wrong with your bike?" he asked, hurrying over.

"The wheel's twisted." Joe was already trying to bend the bike back into shape.

"Ha-ha!" Chet chortled. "Then you are truly helpless to escape the wrath of Morpho! I shall use my monstrous Spork to eat your brains so I can take over your identity!"

He leaned over, pretending to scoop Joe's

brains out of his head with an imaginary spork. Joe just sighed again. Chet loved Morpho even more than the rest of them did. He had first editions of all the comics. He'd seen the Morpho movie seven times. He'd even dressed up as Morpho last Halloween.

"Fine, go ahead and eat my brains," he told Chet with a frown. "It's not like Frank and the others will care. They didn't even notice I wasn't with them anymore!"

Chet shrugged. "They were probably too scared of Morpho to think straight," he suggested. "Anyway, now that you're my victim, you can help me catch them, okay?"

That made Joe feel a little better. "Cool," he said. "I can be your monstrous partner in crime!"

"Yeah!" Chet agreed. "Here, let me help you with your bike. . . ."

The two of them managed to bend the wheel

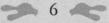

back into shape. Joe climbed on and rode around in a circle to test it.

"It's fine," he reported. "Let's go find the others! Hey, can I wear the Morpho mask for a while?"

Chet shook his head. "No way!" he said. "Sorry, Joe. But this is a limited-edition mask. See? It's got purple ooze on the nose instead of just green ooze."

"Oh yeah." Joe peered at the mask's nose. "That's cool. But how am I supposed to be your

sidekick if I don't have a mask or anything? Come on—I'll be careful, I swear!"

Chet looked worried. "Um, I don't think so," he said. "But I have a better idea. Let's make you a Morph Spork!"

Joe nodded. Morpho's trademark tool was the giant spork that he used to eat brains. It was a combination of a fork and a spoon. Chet had a plastic spork at home, but he hadn't brought it today. So the two of them looked around until they found a branch that was about the right size and shape.

"This should work," Joe said, waving it around like a sword. "I wonder why Morpho uses a spork, anyway."

"Nobody knows," Chet said. He was the expert on everything about Morpho. "Just like nobody knows his original human identity." He grinned. "Hey! Maybe you and Frank should investigate and try to solve the mystery!"

Joe and Frank were known around town for solving mysteries, even though they were only eight and nine years old. Everyone said they were following in their father's footsteps. He was a successful private investigator who'd solved lots of tough cases. But right now Joe wasn't really thinking about that.

"Frank won't be able to solve anything once I eat his brains," he told Chet with a grin. He waved his Spork, then aimed his bike down the trail. "Come on, let's go get them!"

2

A Horrifying Plan

"ROAAAAAAAR!" Chet yelled, running toward his sister Iola.

She screamed and ran away. "Help! Save me from Morpho!" she cried.

Frank grinned as he watched them goof around. The five friends were in Bayport Park. Chet and Joe had caught up to Frank, Iola, and Phil in the woods. Once Morpho and Morpho Jr. had eaten all their friends' brains, the chase was over. Chet was tired of riding his bike, so they'd

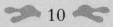

come back to the park to play there.

"Beware the wrath of my Spork!" Joe yelled, waving around his spork-shaped tree branch as he chased Phil. "It's coming for your brains!"

Frank was about to join in the game when he noticed someone coming toward them. *Uh-oh*. It was Adam Ackerman—the biggest bully in Bayport. Adam was in Joe's class at school but was bigger than most of the kids in Frank's grade.

"What are you dummies doing?" Adam asked as he walked toward them. He spotted Chet's Morpho mask and smirked. "Are you in kindergarten, Morton?" he said. "I didn't know people your age still played dress-up like little girls."

"What's wrong with little girls?" Iola challenged Adam, putting her hands on her hips. She was one of the only people who wasn't afraid to stand up to him.

He ignored her, still staring at Chet. "Didn't you hear me?" he said. "I asked you a question, Morton."

"Leave him alone, Adam," Joe said with a frown, clenching his fists at his side.

Frank stepped forward. He could tell that things were getting tense. "It's not a big deal, Adam," he said in a calming voice. "We're just having some fun."

"Yeah," Chet blurted out from behind his mask. "We're getting ready to meet the real Morpho!"

Adam laughed. "The *real* Morpho, huh?" he said sarcastically. "I hate to break it to you, but Morpho is a fictional character. So you can turn

off your night-light and stop worrying about your brains. He's not real."

Iola rolled her eyes. "Duh. Chet just means we're going to meet the Morpho crew at Bayport Comix this weekend."

"Huh?" Adam turned to stare at her. "What are you talking about?"

"Are you just playing dumb?" Joe said. "The actor who played Morpho in the movie and the artist who draws him in the comics are both coming to Bayport Comix on Saturday."

"Yeah! We'll be able to meet them and get their autographs," Chet put in, so excited that he seemed to forget he was talking to Adam.

Phil nodded eagerly. "And don't forget about the special Spork photo booth," he added. "We'll be able to pose with Morpho and the real Spork from the movie. Then they'll do special effects on the photo so it looks like he's really eating our

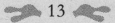

brains! It's going to be really cool—I hope they tell us how the special effects work!"

Frank wasn't surprised to hear him say that. Phil was one of the smartest kids he knew. He loved knowing how things worked, especially technology and anything scientific. In fact, Phil loved that kind of thing just as much as Chet loved Morpho!

"Wow!" Adam said loudly.

Frank glanced over at him. He was sure Adam was about to start making fun of them all more than ever.

To his surprise, though, Adam looked really excited. "Are you guys serious?" he exclaimed. "The real Morpho actor and artist are coming here to Bayport? This weekend?"

"Yeah, the posters have been up at the comics store all week," Joe said with a shrug. "Where've you been?"

"My family was away visiting my grandparents

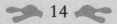 14

this whole week," Adam said. "Oh, man—it's a good thing we got home in time for this! I love Morpho!"

He spun around and raced off without another word. Chet lifted off his mask and watched him go, looking surprised. "Wow," he said. "He seemed really excited. So excited he forgot all about bothering us!"

Frank chuckled. "Yeah," he said. "I guess Morpho is the one thing *everyone* can agree on."

At dinner that night Frank couldn't stop talking about Morpho. Neither could Joe.

"The next Morpho movie is coming out soon," Joe said. "I can't wait to see it!"

"Me neither," Frank agreed, reaching for a piece of bread. "I heard Morpho goes time traveling in this one and tries to eat Abraham Lincoln's brains."

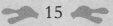 15

Joe snorted. "Figures you'd like that part," he told Frank. "It probably reminds you of social studies class!"

Mr. and Mrs. Hardy traded an amused look. "Sounds like Morpho isn't just gross, he's educational, too," Mr. Hardy quipped.

"Definitely," Frank agreed with a grin.

"Who cares about educational? He's just awesome!" Joe waved his fork in excitement. Unfortunately, there was still a pea stuck on it. It flew off and landed on Aunt Gertrude's plate.

Aunt Gertrude was Mr. Hardy's sister. She'd lived in an apartment in a nearby city for years. But recently she'd grown tired of city living, so Mr. and Mrs. Hardy had invited her to live with them.

She'd moved into the spare room above the garage not long ago.

She frowned as she picked Joe's pea out of her food. "Settle down, please, Joe," she said sternly. "This Morpho character sounds rather silly, if you ask me."

Frank took a drink of water to hide his smile. He got along with Aunt Gertrude pretty well most of the time, so he liked having her live with them. She made great cookies and helped him with his school projects. But Joe wasn't so sure about having her there. Aunt Gertrude scolded him a lot.

"He's not silly at all!" Joe protested. "See, Morpho was once a human just like you and me. But then he got hit in the head by a meteor and morphed into Morpho the Morph Monster, with a huge appetite for human brains! And once he eats your brains, he can morph into your body so your friends and family won't even see him coming!"

"Is this really what passes for entertainment these days?" Aunt Gertrude looked down her long nose at Joe. "I suppose I shouldn't be surprised. But Frank—I'm disappointed that you're interested in something so ridiculous."

Frank shrugged. "It's just for fun, Aunt Gertrude," he said. "Anyway, the event on Saturday should be interesting. Maybe they'll talk about the new movie."

"Saturday?" Aunt Gertrude raised an eyebrow. "You won't have time for that silliness on Saturday. I'm planning to get the whole family tickets to the new exhibit at the art museum that day."

3

Waiting in Line

I can't believe your aunt was going to make you go to some dumb art exhibit instead of seeing Morpho!" Chet exclaimed.

Joe nodded. It was Saturday morning, and he was standing in line outside Bayport Comix with Chet, Frank, Iola, and Phil. There were tons of people ahead of them in line, even though it was only nine thirty and the store didn't open until ten. And more people were arriving all the time. Everyone in town seemed to be excited about the Morpho event!

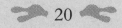

"I know," Joe told Chet. "It's a good thing Mom and Dad talked her into going to the museum next weekend instead." He made a face. "I just wish they'd talk her out of going at all!"

Frank laughed. "The museum won't be so bad," he said. "Anyway, it's a good thing Mom and Dad know how much we love Morpho."

"Yeah," Phil agreed. "It would stink to miss this!"

"Stinky stinky!" a high-pitched voice sang out.

Joe glanced behind him. He'd almost forgotten that Chet and Iola's little sister, Mimi, was with them.

"Hush, Mimi," Iola said with a frown. "You said you'd be good if we let you come."

Joe and Frank traded a doubtful look. Mimi was four years old and kind of weird. She was always trying to tag along everywhere with Chet and Iola. Today she'd begged her parents to let her go to the

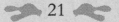

comic book store even though she was scared of Morpho. She wanted to look at the Giggle Girlzies comic books.

But Joe didn't waste much time worrying about Mimi. "I can't wait to see Morpho!" he exclaimed.

Chet nodded. "And the real Spork from the movie!" he added. He pulled his Morpho mask out of his jacket pocket and put it on. "Braaaaaains!" he moaned in his best Morpho voice.

Frank was looking around at the crowd. "There sure are lots of people here. Look, even Adam Ackerman came!"

Joe looked where his brother was pointing.

"Hey, how'd he get ahead of us in line?" he complained.

"Guess he got here sooner," Iola said, peering forward. "Hey, Phil! Isn't that your friend Biff?"

Joe spotted a tall blond kid a few people ahead of Adam in line. Biff lived in Bayport, but he went to the other elementary school. Phil knew him from soccer camp.

"You're right," Phil said. "Biff! Yo, Biff!"

They all called Biff's name. Finally he heard them and turned around and waved. Then he hurried toward them, along with a smaller kid who looked a year or two younger. The second kid was holding a Morpho mask.

"Hi," Biff said. "Everyone, this is my cousin Colin from Northtown. He came for the Morpho event."

"Yeah, I heard about it on MorphoNet. I'm the world's hugest Morpho fan!" Colin exclaimed, hopping up and down on one foot and twirling

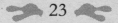

his mask. "I saw the Morpho movie in the theater fifteen times, and I have three DVD copies, plus every comic ever printed and a life-size Morpho poster in my room. I'm probably the leading expert on Morpho in the entire universe!"

Frank laughed. "Uh-oh, Chet," he joked. "Sounds like you have some competition!"

Colin looked at Chet. "Whoa! Is that the limited-edition Morpho mask with deluxe purple slime?" he asked.

Joe looked at Chet's mask, then at Colin's. They were almost identical. But Colin's only had green slime on the nose, and Chet's had green *and* purple slime.

"Yeah," Chet said proudly. "I wore it for Halloween this year."

"Awesome! Let me know if you ever want to sell it," Colin said.

"No way, it's not for sale," Chet said. "Sorry!"

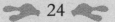 24

"That's okay." Colin shrugged and started hopping on the other foot. "I bet someone will put one up for sale on MorphoNet soon."

He put on his mask. Then he started walking around with his arms out, just like Morpho.

Chet grinned. "That's pretty good. Can you do the Morpho roar?"

"Sure!" Colin took a deep breath. "ROAAAAAR!"

"ROAAAAAR!" Chet roared back.

"No!" Mimi shrieked, covering her ears. "Stop it!"

She hid behind Iola. Iola rolled her eyes. "It's just Chet," she told her sister. "Besides, you were the one who wanted to come today!"

Mimi started crying. "It's too scary!" she sobbed. "I only wanted to see the Giggle Girlzies!"

Chet took off his mask, and he and Iola tried to calm Mimi down. But she wouldn't stop crying.

"We'd better get back to our place in line," Biff said. "Come on, Colin."

"See you guys inside," Colin said. Then he and Biff hurried off.

"Are you happy now?" Chet asked Mimi. "You scared them away."

Joe laughed. "Yeah. Mimi's way scarier than Morpho!"

Mimi stopped crying and scowled at Joe. "Am not!" she yelled. "I'm a Giggle Girlzie!"

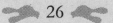

Iola rolled her eyes. "Will you stop complaining if we play Giggle Girlzies with you while we wait?"

"Yes!" Mimi squealed. "Giggle Girlzies! Giggle Girlzies!"

Chet made her promise to be good for the whole rest of the day. Then they all started giggling loudly. The people in line nearby gave them funny looks. But Joe figured it would be worth it if it kept Mimi out of their hair once the Morpho event started.

Ten a.m. seemed to take forever to arrive. But finally there was a murmur from the front of the line. A second later the doors swung open.

"It's time!" Joe exclaimed.

He rushed forward with the others. As soon as he got a look at the inside of the comic book store, he grinned. The place was Morphoed to the max! There were several life-size cutouts of

Morpho standing here and there. Huge posters covered every inch of wall space. Stuffed Morpho toys, plastic Sporks, and all kinds of other Morpho merchandise were everywhere.

"This is awesome!" Chet cried.

"Yeah!" Frank exclaimed.

"No!" Mimi wailed. "It's too scary! I want to leave—*right now*!"

4

Meeting Morpho

Iola groaned. "We can't leave, Mimi!" she said.

"You promised to be good," Chet reminded her.

"I don't care!" Mimi sobbed. "I—" Suddenly she stopped crying. "Hey!" she exclaimed happily. "It's Janie!"

She waved across the store. A girl her age with bright red pigtails waved back. She was standing with a teenage girl.

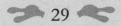

"That's Janie's big sister," Chet said. "Come on, Mimi, let's go talk to her."

Moments later he returned—without Mimi. "Did Janie's sister say she'd watch her?" Iola asked.

"Uh-huh." Chet looked happy. "They're back in the corner of the store with the girly books."

Frank wasn't paying much attention to them. There was too much cool Morpho stuff to look at! Unfortunately, it was getting harder and harder to see it all as more people crowded into the store.

He looked toward the back wall. There was a door in the middle marked Employees Only. On the left side of the door was the kids' section of the store. On the other side there was a temporary wooden stage.

"What time does the show start?" he asked.

Joe stood on tiptoe to read the sign near the front door. "It says the special guests appear at ten thirty," he said. "We have time to look around first."

"Let's go check out the newest Morpho comic book," Phil suggested.

Frank followed Phil toward a rack of comics nearby. When they got there, he looked back. He saw lots of people, but not Joe or Chet or Iola.

"Oops," he said. "I think we lost the others."

Phil shrugged and reached for a Morpho comic. "We'll find them when the show starts."

"I hope so." Frank glanced around. "This place is packed!"

He and Phil were still looking at the comics when Biff found them. "Hi," he said. "This is cool, isn't it?"

"Yeah," Frank agreed. "Where's your cousin?"

"I'm not sure. We got separated." Biff looked around. He was taller than a lot of the kids in the store, so Frank guessed he had a pretty good view. "He's probably over by the stage staking out a front-row spot. He won't want to miss

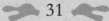

getting a great view of his idol, Morpho!"

Phil laughed. "Yeah. He seemed pretty excited."

"The rest of us might be Morpho fans," Biff said with a grin, "but Colin's a Morpho *superfan*!"

The three of them were still hanging out near the comic rack when they heard a commotion from the back of the store. "Come on," Biff said. "It must be starting!"

Frank dropped the comic book he was holding. Then he rushed toward the back of the store with the others. When they reached the crowd around the stage, Frank spotted Joe standing with Iola. He, Phil, and Biff joined them just as Morpho himself burst out from the Employees Only door.

"ROAAAAAAAAAAAAAR!" he yelled so loudly that Frank's ears hurt.

Most of the crowd roared back or yelled with excitement. But then Frank heard an even louder shriek of fear.

 32

"Uh-oh," he muttered.

Glancing to the left, he was just in time to see Mimi and her little friend race into the back through the Employees Only door, screaming with terror. Janie's sister rushed after them, looking worried.

Iola saw them, too. "Oh no," she moaned. "Where's Chet? We should probably go after her."

"Forget it," Phil told her. "That older girl babysits Mimi sometimes, right? She'll be able to find them."

Iola still looked worried. But she nodded. "I guess you're right."

Up on the stage, the man in the Morpho costume reached up and lifted off his mask. Frank was surprised by what he looked like underneath. Morpho was big and beefy, like a superstrong bodybuilder. But the actor who played him looked like a normal guy. He was actually kind of wimpy-looking.

But when he spoke, he had a deep voice. "Thanks for coming, everyone," he said. "My name's Jack, and I'm lucky to play Morpho in the movies. Now I'd like to introduce you to the guy who first brought him to life in the comics we all know and love. Come on out, Dave!"

The artist hurried out and said hello. He looked like a regular guy too.

"Neither of them looks much like the Morpho type," Joe whispered to Frank.

"I know what you mean," Frank murmured back. "But I guess that's what Morpho is all about, right? He can morph to look like anyone at all, like those guys. Or us. Or even Mimi."

He shot another look toward the door. There was still no sign of the girls.

But he didn't worry about that for long. The actor and artist sat down on stools and started talking about the history of Morpho. It was really interesting. First the artist showed some sketches. Then an assistant brought out a few props from the movie.

A kid near the front of the crowd raised his hand. "How did you come up with the idea for the Morph Spork?" he asked.

"Great question." The artist smiled, then turned to signal to the assistant. "Bring out the Spork, will you?" he called.

There was a murmur of excitement from the audience. Everyone was eager to see the real Spork from the Morpho movie!

"I wonder if it'll look smaller in person, like the actor does?" Joe said to the others.

Iola giggled. "I guess we're about to find out!"

A second later the assistant reappeared. But he wasn't carrying the Spork—or anything else. He hurried up to Dave and whispered something in his ear.

The artist frowned. "Are you sure?" he said. "Let me look."

He hurried offstage and through the door. "Don't worry, kids," the actor said. "He'll be back soon with the Spork."

The artist did come back soon. But he wasn't

holding the Spork. The owner of the comic book store, Mr. Roberts, was with him. They both looked worried.

"Where's the Spork?" someone in the crowd yelled eagerly.

"I'm afraid we have a problem," Mr. Roberts announced. "Morpho's Morph Spork is missing!"

5

Where's the Spork?

O h no!" Joe exclaimed. He couldn't believe his ears. How could the Morph Spork be missing?

Everyone else was surprised too. Just about the whole audience started talking at once.

"This is terrible," Phil said. "Morpho's nothing without his Spork!"

Joe glanced at the stage. Mr. Roberts was talking to Dave and Jack. All three of them looked upset.

Joe couldn't blame them. This was bad news.

"Attention, please!" Dave called out. "We really need that Spork back."

Jack nodded. "We know there are lots of enthusiastic Morpho fans here. But stealing is wrong."

"Do you think someone stole the Spork?" Frank whispered.

Joe shrugged. "What else could have happened to it?"

Meanwhile, a kid near the front raised his hand. "Who cares if the Spork is gone?" he called out. "I read on MorphoNet that there's going to be a new SuperSpork in the next movie!"

There was a murmur of interest from the crowd. But Jack shook his head.

"We still need the old Spork," he said. "We're supposed to auction it off for charity after this tour is over."

Mr. Roberts looked more worried than ever.

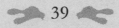

"Whoever took that Spork needs to return it right away," he said. "Until it's back, this event is on hold."

"No way!" someone cried. A few other people protested too.

But Mr. Roberts didn't say anything else. He headed out through the Employees Only door, followed by Jack and Dave.

"This stinks," Iola declared.

Joe nodded and looked around. The store was in an uproar. Everyone was talking about what had happened. Some people were also casting suspicious looks around at everyone else.

"You know what I think?" Phil said.

Joe glanced at him. "What?"

"I think this sounds like a mystery."

Iola gasped. "You're right!" she exclaimed. "You guys should investigate!"

Joe shrugged. "We don't need to. I already know who took that Spork."

"Who?" Biff asked.

"Who else?" Joe said. "It has to be Adam Ackerman."

Frank frowned. "Why does it have to be him?"

"Don't you remember our first mystery?" Joe couldn't believe his brother didn't get it. "When all that money disappeared at the arcade, Adam turned out to be the thief. This is just like that time."

"Adam *is* bad news," Iola said. "He steals people's lunches at school all the time."

Joe nodded. "Let's go find him and tell him to

give the Spork back before Mr. Roberts cancels the whole Morpho day!"

"Hold on!" Frank said. "None of us likes Adam. But we can't just accuse him of stealing the Spork with no proof."

"Why not?" Joe asked impatiently. "We know he did it!"

"No, we don't," Frank said. "Dad always says it's important not to jump to conclusions, right?"

"Yeah, I guess he says that sometimes," Joe agreed reluctantly. "So what?"

"So, what if it *wasn't* Adam?" Frank said. "We shouldn't get too focused on a suspect until we're sure. Even if Adam *is* a pretty good suspect."

"I think he might be right, Joe," Phil said. "That makes sense."

"Yeah," Iola agreed. "There are tons of people here, and we don't know all of them. Some

of them might be just as rotten as Adam."

Joe still thought Adam was the thief. But he realized his brother and the others were right.

"Okay," he said. "Even if it *is* Adam, I guess we need some proof. Otherwise, he'll never confess."

Frank smiled. "Good point. I'm not saying it's *not* Adam. He's definitely at the top of the suspect list. But we need some evidence or it's just our word against his."

"So how do you find evidence?" Biff asked, looking interested.

"We usually start out with the six *W*s," Frank explained. "That means we ask Who, What, When, Where, Why, and How and try to . . ."

Joe didn't hear the rest of what his brother said. He'd just turned to scan the store.

"Check it out!" he interrupted, pointing. "Adam Ackerman is trying to sneak out the front door right now!"

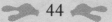

Looking for Suspects

"**W**ait!" Frank yelled to Joe.

But it was too late. Joe was already rushing across the store toward Adam. Iola was right behind him, but Biff and Phil got left behind.

Frank hurried after his brother. He caught up just as he and Iola reached Adam.

"I knew it!" Joe exclaimed, pointing at Adam. "You were the one who took that Spork, weren't you? Just admit it!"

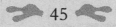

Adam turned toward him with a scowl. "*I* knew it," he said. "That's why I was leaving. You guys are always accusing me when bad stuff happens!"

Iola folded her arms across her chest. "That's only because you're usually guilty," she told him.

He glared at her, then at Frank and Joe. "I know you goody-goodies think I'm always the bad guy," he said. "But I swear I didn't take that Spork. I'd never do that to Morpho!"

"Then who took it?" Joe challenged him.

"How should I know?" Adam shot back.

There was a big strong man standing by the

front door. Frank noticed him looking their way with a frown.

"Hey, you guys," Frank said quietly. "Let's back off, okay?"

"Not until Adam gives back the Spork," Iola said.

Frank looked at Adam. That's when he realized something. He grabbed Joe and pulled him aside, leaving Adam to argue with Iola.

"Hold on a second," Frank whispered. "If Adam took the Spork, where is it? He isn't carrying a bag or anything."

Joe looked at Adam. Then he shrugged. "He could've hidden it somewhere so he could come back and get it later," he pointed out. "That's what he did with the money that time at the arcade."

"I guess," Frank said. "But then why would he leave the store?"

Joe shrugged. He looked kind of stubborn.

Frank could see that his brother was convinced that Adam was the thief. But was he really the culprit?

Just then Adam pushed past them, heading back into the main part of the store. "I changed my mind," he said. "I'm not going to let a bunch of creeps chase me away. I'm here to see Morpho."

"Nobody's going to see Morpho again if that Spork doesn't turn up," Joe said.

But Adam was already too far away to hear him. Joe sighed.

"Don't worry," Frank told him. "If Adam did it, we'll figure it out."

Iola came over just in time to hear him. "Yeah," she said. "You two always solve the case!"

Joe smiled. "That's true."

Frank stared around the store. There were pictures of the Spork everywhere. Where could the real one be? Who would be mean enough to steal it?

"I wish I had a way to take notes," he said. He had

forgotten his trusty reporter's notebook at home. That was where he always wrote up their cases.

Joe rolled his eyes. "You always want to take notes," he said. "But there's no time for stuff like that. Let's just start interviewing people. Somebody must have seen something suspicious."

Frank hesitated. He thought they should begin at the beginning—by talking about the six *W*s. But maybe Joe was right. The store was really crowded. It seemed impossible that someone had stolen the Spork without anyone seeing them do it.

"Okay," he said. "I guess we could talk to a few people and see what we find out."

Joe looked at Iola. "Want to help?"

"Sure," she said, sounding a little distracted. "But I'd better go find Chet first. I want to see if he knows where Mimi is."

Frank nodded. He hadn't seen Mimi since she'd run out through the back door. Come to think of

it, he hadn't seen Chet in even longer than that.

"Okay," he said. "We'll meet up with you later."

Iola disappeared into the crowd. Frank and Joe wandered around, looking for someone to interview. First they talked to a bored-looking girl with purple hair. She said she thought it was all a publicity stunt and that the Morpho people knew exactly where the Spork was right now.

Frank didn't think that was very likely, so he and Joe moved on. They asked a couple of teenage boys if they'd noticed anyone suspicious hanging

around. The teenagers said they'd seen a shady-looking guy dressed in black sneaking into the back room. Frank started to get excited, but then he realized they were just teasing them.

"This isn't going very well," Joe said as the teenagers wandered away snorting with laughter.

Before Frank could answer, he spotted Biff and his cousin Colin hurrying toward them. Colin looked more hyper than ever.

"Can you believe this?" Colin exclaimed when he reached them, waving both hands in the air. "I can't believe the Spork is gone!"

"Me neither," Biff agreed. "Who do you think took it?"

"We're not sure yet," Joe began. "We think—"

"It's extra serious because this is, like, *the* Spork!" Colin interrupted. "It's the very first one they made—the one Morpho was holding in the movie when he got captured by the commandos.

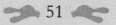 51

That makes it a superspecial and one-of-a-kind collector's item."

"Really?" Joe said. "No wonder those Morpho guys looked so upset."

Before Frank could say anything, they all heard Mr. Roberts calling for attention again. When the room quieted down a little, he said he had another announcement to make.

"We really need that Spork back, and soon," he said with a serious look on his face. "If it's not back before three o'clock at the latest, the rest of today's Morpho event will be canceled."

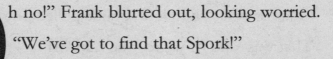

7

Another Mystery

O h no!" Frank blurted out, looking worried. "We've got to find that Spork!"

"Yeah!" Biff exclaimed. "This is really getting serious."

"Don't worry, you guys," Joe said. "We'll find the Spork!"

He looked around for Adam, but he didn't see him. It was hard to spot anyone in the store just then. Everyone was milling around, looking upset and talking about Mr. Roberts's announcement.

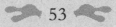

"Even if you don't find it, it's no big deal," Colin said. "They're having a Morpho event at the comics store in my town next month. You could all come there—it's only a two-hour drive."

"We should still try to find it," Joe said. "Let's split up. We can talk to more people that way."

"Cool," Biff said. "Come on, Colin. Let's go find someone to interview."

As soon as they left, Frank pulled Joe aside. "That was kind of weird," he said. "If Colin could go see Morpho in his own town in a month, why'd he bother to come all the way to Bayport?"

Joe shrugged. "Colin's a superfan, remember? He probably goes to all the Morpho events he can." He looked around. "Anyway, we have bigger problems right now. We have to figure out what happened to that Spork!"

"Do you still think Adam took it?" Frank asked.

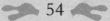

"Yeah," Joe said. "But you were right. We have to investigate everyone, just in case."

Frank smiled. Joe knew why: His brother loved being right.

"Okay," Frank said. "Let's get back to interviewing people."

They parted ways. As Joe wandered into the crowd, all around him he could hear people talking about the missing Spork. But nobody sounded as if they knew what might have happened to it.

Then he spotted Adam near the comics rack. He was leaning against the rack as he paged through the new Morpho comic.

Joe narrowed his eyes and watched him for a few seconds. But Adam didn't move. He just kept reading the comic book.

Finally Joe decided to move on. He could keep an eye on Adam while he talked to people.

He interviewed several kids about the missing

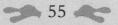

Spork, but nobody had anything useful to tell him. Just as he finished talking to a skinny girl with braces, he saw Frank coming toward him.

"Did you find out anything?" Frank asked.

Joe shook his head. "Nothing useful. What about you?"

"Maybe," Frank said. "A couple of kids said they saw someone in a Morpho mask sneaking into the back room a few minutes after the event started."

"A Morpho mask?" Joe looked around. Without even trying, he spotted at least four or five masks

like the ones Chet and Colin had brought. "That doesn't narrow it down much. Besides, isn't the bathroom back through that back door? Maybe that's where that mystery person was going."

"Maybe. But the kids I talked to thought it was weird, since the person in the mask left right when the artist started showing all those cool sketches." Frank shrugged. "Anyway, it's the only clue we have so far."

Joe thought about what Frank had said. Those Morpho masks were kind of expensive. Anyone who had one was probably a big fan. Why would someone like that want to miss part of this event?

"I guess that is a pretty good clue," he told Frank. Suddenly he remembered the teenagers who'd tried to trick him with the fake-out story. "Wait," he added. "Who were the kids who told you? Are they reliable witnesses?"

That was a term he'd heard his father use lots

of times. A reliable witness was someone who was likely to be telling the truth.

"I'm not sure," Frank said. "It wasn't anyone we know. They said they were from out of town."

Joe frowned. "What if they're making it all up? They could even be friends of Adam's. He could have told them to cover for him."

"I guess." Frank sounded doubtful. "Anyway, we should try to find out if anyone else saw what they said they saw."

"Right," Joe said. "Dad has a word for that, right? A cardboard witness, or something."

"I think it's a *corroborating* witness," Frank said.

Joe shrugged. Frank was always better than he was at vocabulary words. "Whatever. We should figure out who was near that door and ask them."

"I know!" Frank looked excited. "I just remembered—Biff said his cousin would prob-ably be in the front row when the Morpho guys

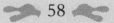

came out. He would have a great view of that Employees Only door from there, right?"

"Right!" Now Joe was excited too. This could be the clue they needed! "Let's go find Colin!"

They looked around. The store was still really crowded, so it was hard to see anyone more than a few feet away.

Joe led the way into the crowd, searching for Colin. He and Frank had only gone a few yards when they heard Chet calling their names.

"Hi, guys," Chet said breathlessly, hurrying over to them. "I've been looking all over for you!"

He looked worried. Joe thought he knew why.

"Don't worry," he told Chet. "We're trying to find Morpho's Spork."

"Okay," Chet said. "Um, but have you seen Mimi lately?"

"Mimi?" Frank shook his head. "I haven't seen her since she got scared and ran out with her friend."

Chet bit his lip, looking more worried than ever. "Neither has anyone else," he said. "Janie's sister chased them through the Employees Only door, but she couldn't find them anywhere. They're missing!"

8

Sidetracked

Joe groaned. "Are you serious?" he asked Chet. "This really isn't a good time for Mimi to pull one of her goofy stunts."

Frank knew how his brother felt. He really wanted to keep searching for the Spork. But he knew they'd better help find Mimi and her friend first.

"So nobody has seen them since they ran away?" he asked Chet.

"Nobody we've talked to so far." Chet glanced

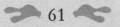

around anxiously. "I'm going to go check the girly section again. Maybe they're sitting under a table reading Giggle Girlzies comics or something."

As he hurried off Frank glanced at Joe. "Come on," he said. "Let's go talk to that guy at the front door."

"What guy?" Joe asked.

"He looked like a guard or something. I noticed him watching when you were arguing with Adam a little while ago."

Frank headed toward the front door with Joe right behind him. When they got there, the same big guy was standing just inside the door.

Just then a pair of teenage girls hurried toward the exit. Both of them were carrying shopping bags.

"Pardon me, young ladies," the guard said. "I'll need to check your bags."

"Why?" one of the girls asked. "All that's in there are our new Morpho comics."

"Yeah," the other girl said. "We paid for them."

The guard shrugged. "I'm supposed to check everyone's bags for that missing movie prop," he explained.

"Oh, okay." The first girl held up her bag. "It's not in here."

The guard looked in both girls' bags, then waved them through. When he was finished, Frank stepped up to him.

"Excuse me," he said politely. "We're looking for two little girls."

The guard waved his hand at the door. "You mean those two who just left?"

"No," Joe said. "Way younger than that. These girls are about four years old. Did you notice if they left the store this way?"

The guard raised one eyebrow. "Four-year-old

girls?" he said. "Nope, haven't seen any of those leave. And I definitely would have noticed. This isn't exactly that kind of crowd!"

He chuckled and glanced into the store. Frank looked too. He saw what the guard meant. Most of the people in the store were their age or older. And only a few of them were girls.

"So you're sure no little girls have left?" he asked.

"I'm positive," the guard said. "Good luck finding them."

Just then a teenage boy came along wanting to leave. The guard turned to check his bags, and Frank and Joe wandered back into the store.

"Okay, so we know Mimi and her friend are still in here somewhere," Joe said.

"Not necessarily," Frank pointed out. "The last time anyone saw them, they were running into that back room. There's probably a door back there, too."

"Oh, right!" Joe said. "Come on, let's go look."

Soon they were walking through the Employees Only door. "This feels weird," Frank said. "We're not employees."

Joe didn't pay any attention. He was already in the hallway on the other side of the door.

Frank shrugged and followed. He looked up and down the hallway. To the left was the bathroom. To the right were two doors. One was closed and said Storage on it. The other was partway open and said Lounge. Frank could hear voices coming from behind that door. He guessed it was where the Morpho people were waiting.

"Look," Joe whispered, pointing to a third door. It was bigger and said Exit on it.

When they pushed it open, they saw a narrow alley. Across the way were the back doors of the stores on the next block. There was a Dumpster behind each door. A large bird was pecking at something on the ground near one of the

Dumpsters. Other than that, Frank saw no signs of life.

"Mimi wouldn't hang around out here for long," he said, wrinkling his nose. "It smells kind of gross."

Joe nodded. "Still, she might have left this way and then wandered off down the alley looking for ice cream or something."

Frank peered down the alley. At the end he could see the street. "Maybe," he said. "Let's go inside and see if Chet found anything."

He started to turn around. But Joe was staring at something.

"Do you see that?" he said, sounding excited.

"What? The bird?" Frank glanced that way.

"No!" Joe rushed out into the alley, heading for one of the Dumpsters on the other side.

Frank sighed. Joe was always getting distracted. But they didn't have time for that now. "Come back!" he called. "We need to keep looking for Mimi."

Joe ignored him. He was already stepping up onto a box to reach the top of the Dumpster. When he looked inside the Dumpster, he let out a shout. Then he grabbed something out of it and started waving it around.

"Check it out!" he yelled. "I just found Morpho's Spork!"

9

Mask Attack

Joe jumped down from the Dumpster, feeling excited. He couldn't believe he'd just found the Spork! He raced over to the door, waving the Spork over his head.

"Come on!" he said to a surprised-looking Frank. "Let's go give this back!"

They ran inside. The door to the lounge was still half open. Joe pushed through it. Dave and Jack were inside, along with their assistant. Mr. Roberts wasn't there.

"Hey, you guys!" Joe exclaimed. "Look what we found!"

Dave gasped. "The Spork! Is it all right?"

He grabbed the Spork from Joe and started examining it. Meanwhile, Jack stared at both Hardys.

"Where did you find this, boys?" he asked sternly.

"It was in the Dumpster in the alley out back," Frank explained.

Joe nodded. "We were looking out there for someone, and I saw it sticking out."

"Oh, really?" Now the actor sounded suspicious. "You just happened to be looking for someone in the alley?"

Dave looked up. "I think we'd better go talk to Mr. Roberts about this."

Joe gasped as he realized what was happening. The Morpho people thought he and Frank had stolen the Spork themselves!

 70

"No!" he blurted out. "It wasn't us, we swear!"

Dave handed the Spork to the assistant. "Don't let this out of your sight," he warned. Then he glared at the boys. "You two had better come with us."

Dave and Jack hurried out of the room. Joe traded a helpless glance with Frank.

"They think we're the thieves!" he whispered.

"I know." Frank looked worried. "Come on, we need to talk to them."

By the time they caught up, the two men were out in the main part of the store. "Please!" Joe said. "You have to believe us. We aren't the ones who took the Spork."

"Hmm," Dave said. "If you didn't take the Spork, who did?"

Before Joe could answer, he noticed Adam standing nearby. Adam had just overheard what they'd said.

 71

"I knew it!" Adam spoke up loudly, pointing to Frank and Joe. "Those two are the town troublemakers!"

"What?" Joe squawked.

But Dave seemed to believe Adam. "Is that right, son?" he asked. "I'm glad you let us know." He glanced at Jack. "Stay with them," he told the actor. "I'll find Roberts and tell him to call the police—and these guys' parents." Then he hurried off into the crowded store.

Joe couldn't believe this was happening. How dare Adam accuse them of being troublemakers?

"You shouldn't listen to him!" he told Jack, pointing at Adam. "*He's* the only troublemaker around here! Ask anyone!"

Adam smirked and wandered away. Joe looked around for someone to vouch for them. But there was no sign of Chet, Iola, Phil, Biff, or anyone else they knew.

 72

"Where is everyone?" Frank said, sounding nervous.

"They're probably all still looking for Mimi," Joe replied. "I wonder where she is, anyway?"

"What if *she's* the one who took the Spork?" Frank said. "She's really scared of Morpho. Maybe Mimi thought throwing away his Spork would mean he couldn't eat her brains."

"Yeah, that sounds like her," Joe said.

Jack was listening, looking skeptical. "Look, it won't do you any good to blame someone else," he said. "I'm sure the police can get to the bottom of things."

Just then Mr. Roberts came rushing over. Dave was right behind him.

"There they are," Dave said, pointing to the Hardys.

Mr. Roberts looked surprised. "*These* are the boys you were talking about?" he exclaimed. "I think there's been some mistake. Frank and Joe Hardy are good kids."

Jack and Dave traded a look. They still seemed doubtful.

"I've known these boys for years," Mr. Roberts went on. "Their father, too—he's a top-notch private investigator, and these two are pretty good little detectives themselves. You should see the write-up they got in the newspaper when they solved a shoplifting case at a store down the block."

"Thanks, Mr. Roberts," Frank said.

"Yeah," Joe added. "We've been trying to figure out who took the Spork."

Mr. Roberts finally convinced the Morpho people to let the Hardys keep investigating to find out who'd really stolen the Spork.

"All right, but you'd better hurry," Dave said at last. "Even though the Spork is back, we're not going on with the show until we've caught the thief."

Jack checked his watch. "You still have until three o'clock."

"Okay," Joe said. "Come on, Frank. Let's go back out and look for clues in the alley."

Soon the two of them were back at the Dumpster. Frank started looking on the ground for clues while Joe climbed the ladder again.

At first he didn't see anything inside the Dumpster except trash. Yuck! This Dumpster belonged to a restaurant, so the trash was filled with old food—and was pretty gross.

Then Joe spotted something sticking out from a pile of discarded rice. He reached over and grabbed it. When he pulled it out, he gasped.

"I found a Morpho mask!" he called to Frank.

He climbed down and handed the mask to his brother. Frank wiped off most of the rice, holding the mask carefully by its green-goo-covered nose.

"This makes me think about what those kids

told me," he said. "They said they saw someone in a Morpho mask sneaking through the Employees Only door, remember?"

Joe nodded. "Whoever was wearing this mask probably grabbed the Spork out of the back room," he guessed.

"Right," Frank agreed. "Then they hid it in the Dumpster along with this mask, and sneaked back inside."

"So all we have to do is figure out who's missing their Morpho mask," Joe said.

Frank looked worried. "That won't be easy. There were at least ten or fifteen people with those masks here today. I'm not even sure I remember all of them."

Joe shrugged. "At least it's a clue," he said. "Come on, let's go back in."

The two of them headed inside and started checking everyone they'd seen earlier with one of the masks. They'd checked several people already when Joe spotted Biff's cousin.

"Hey, Colin," he said, hurrying over. "Where's your Morpho mask?"

Colin reached around and pulled out the mask sticking half out of his back pocket. "Right here,"

he said, twirling it around by its green-and-purple nose. "Why do you ask?"

"Um, no reason." Joe didn't have time to explain right now. They still had more masks to check.

But before he and Frank could move on, they heard a shout of relief from somewhere nearby. "That sounded like Chet," Frank said.

Joe looked toward the shout. He saw Chet coming through the Employees Only door, dragging Mimi with one hand and her friend Janie with the other.

"Where'd you find them?" Joe asked, hurrying over with Frank at his heels.

"We were hiding from the monsters!" Mimi informed him.

"They were hiding in the bathroom," Chet said with a sigh. "Janie's sister just found them in there. She's calling her parents to let them know."

 78

"Whew!" Frank said. "That's a relief."

"Yeah." Chet dropped the little girls' hands. They ran off toward the nearest Giggle Girlzies display.

Then Chet reached into his jacket pocket. Pulling out a tissue, he mopped his face.

Joe's eyes widened as he noticed something. Namely, something that *wasn't* sticking out of Chet's pocket anymore.

"Hey, Chet," he blurted out. "Where's your Morpho mask?"

10

Secret File #5:
A Surprising Solution

Chet gasped. "Oh no!" he cried. "My mask!"

He searched his jacket pockets. Then he checked his jeans pockets. But the mask wasn't in any of them.

Frank noticed the Morpho people turning to look at them from nearby. Had they heard Chet just now? Would they figure out what was going on and accuse him of the crime?

Chet looked frantic as he searched his pockets again. "I can't believe I lost it!" he exclaimed.

"Where'd you have it last?" Joe sounded worried too.

"I know I had it when Morpho first came out." Chet glanced toward the stage. "I put it on and roared with everyone else. But then I took it off so I could hear better."

"Did you stick it back in your jacket pocket?" Frank asked.

"I think so." Chet stuck his hand in his pocket one more time. "But maybe I dropped it over there. I'll go check."

He rushed off toward the stage. Frank and Joe stared at each other.

"Do you think Chet could be the thief?" Frank asked.

"No way!" Joe said. "Chet wouldn't do something like that."

Frank bit his lip. "I can't believe one of our

best friends could be a thief either," he said slowly. "But the evidence . . ."

"The evidence is wrong," Joe said firmly. "Chet didn't do it. It was probably Adam, like I thought all along."

Frank wished he could be that certain. But every time he thought about their clues, they all pointed in one direction—straight at Chet.

"How can you be so sure?" he asked his brother. "Neither of us saw Chet during the whole time the Spork was missing. Then we found that mask at the scene of the crime. And now it looks like it's got to be Chet's. What else could it all mean? The answer is as plain as the nose on your face."

Joe gasped. "That's it!" he cried.

"Huh?" Frank wasn't sure what his brother was talking about.

Joe looked excited. He spun around and waved

his arms at Dave, Jack, and Mr. Roberts. "I just figured it out!" he called to them. "I know who really took that Morph Spork!"

Frank felt worried. Was Joe going to blame Adam again? They didn't have any proof.

By now Joe had everyone's attention. "Who was it, Joe?" Mr. Roberts asked.

Joe smiled grimly. "It was . . . ," he began.

Then he spun around and pointed—right at Biff's cousin Colin!

• • • •

"Are you sure you don't want to write up the case?" Frank asked. "You're the one who solved it."

It was several hours later. Frank and Joe were in their tree house. Joe was lounging on the floor cushions while Frank stood in front of the whiteboard where they wrote up all their cases.

"No thanks," Joe said. "You can do it."

"Okay." Frank jotted down a few notes. Then he glanced at Joe again. "I still can't believe you figured it out."

Joe grinned modestly. "You helped," he said. "It was what you said about the answer being as plain as the nose on my face. That reminded me of those masks."

"That's when you remembered that the mask we found in the trash only had green ooze on its nose, right?" Frank said.

"Right." Joe leaned back against the wall. "But

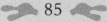

Chet's mask had green *and* purple ooze. So I knew that couldn't have been his mask. And then I remembered that when we asked Colin about his mask, he pulled out one with green and purple ooze. . . ."

Frank nodded, thinking back. "Even though we knew his mask only had the green ooze," he finished. "I should have noticed that."

"Me too," Joe said with a shrug. "I guess that's why Dad is always telling us to keep our eyes open."

"He's also always telling us to follow the evidence," Frank said. "That's what you did today!"

Joe sat up. "I guess so," he said. "But you were following the evidence too, and you were ready to blame Chet for the whole thing. It was only because my gut told me Chet wasn't the thief that I thought harder and remembered about the masks."

"Maybe." Frank shrugged. "I guess sometimes there's more to solving mysteries than just cold, hard facts."

"Yeah," Joe agreed. "Anyway, I'm glad Colin confessed so we know how he did it."

Frank wrote something else on the board. "Me too," he said. "He really wanted that special Spork to add to his collection. When he noticed nobody was in the back room, he put on his mask, sneaked back there, and snatched that Spork. He realized he wouldn't be able to sneak it back through the store, so he tossed it in the Dumpster along with his mask. He figured he'd pick them both up later after things cooled off."

"Yeah. But once he sneaked back inside and found out we were investigating, he got worried," Joe went on. "Especially later, when he heard we'd found his mask."

"So he saw that Chet was distracted and sneaked his mask out of his pocket so he'd have a mask alibi—not to mention the cool special-edition mask he wanted," Frank finished. "Good

thing you figured out the ooze thing, or he might have gotten away with it!"

Joe sighed. "I feel bad for Biff. He was really upset when he found out what Colin did."

"I feel kind of bad for Colin, too," Frank said. "He didn't mean to hurt anyone."

"Uh-huh," Joe agreed. "He seemed nice otherwise. I hope he learns a lesson from this."

Frank finished filling out the whiteboard, then stepped back to take a look.

"There," he said. "How does that look?"

Joe grinned. "Like a monster of a case—closed!"

SECRET FILES CASE #5 SOLVED!

JOE IS EXCITED ABOUT HIS NEW COMIC BOOK. . . .

Check it out! It's Morpho #87— hot off the presses.

Cool!

MORPHO

Boys! Time for dinner!

Guess I'll have to read this later.

MORPHO

Hurry, I'm hungry!

AT DINNER JOE TELLS EVERYONE ABOUT HIS NEW COMIC BOOK.

Morpho's the coolest!

Sounds pretty silly to me. You boys should read something more wholesome.

AFTER DINNER . . .

Please clear the table, boys.

Okay, Dad.

GROAN!